THE DOG IN THE DIAMOND COLLAR

THE DOG IN THE DIAMOND COLLAR

REBECCA LISLE

Illustrated by Tim Archbold

ANDERSEN PRESS · LONDON

First published in 2006 by
Andersen Press Limited,
20 Vauxhall Bridge Road, London SW1V 2SA
www.andersenpress.co.uk

This edition published in 2014

British Library Cataloguing in Publication Data
available
ISBN-10: 1 84270 366 8
ISBN-13: 978 184 270 366 3

Printed and bound in China

1
The Dog Arrives

Joe was hanging upside down from the tree house when he saw the dog.

'There's a dog in our garden,' he said. 'He's black and white. D'you think he's lost?'

'Yes,' said Laurie.

'That's lucky,' said Theo. He was the youngest and only allowed on the lowest branches of the tree. He scrambled down. 'I want a dog.'

'So do I,' said Laurie, following him.

They surrounded the little dog and patted him. He was a nice dog. He lay on his back and showed them his pink tummy and wagged his tail.

'He's got diamonds on his collar,' said Theo. 'That's lucky. I like diamonds.'

'Don't be silly, dogs don't wear diamonds,' said Joe. He was the eldest.

'They do if they're rich,' said Theo, hugging the dog. 'I'm going to keep him.'

'*We're* going to keep him, you mean,' said Laurie.

'There isn't a name tag,' said Joe. He examined the dog's collar. 'We'll have to look after him until someone claims him.'

'What shall we call him?' asked Laurie.

'I'm going to call him Clinky,' said Theo. 'Clinky Monkey.'

'He isn't a monkey. Don't be stupid!' Joe said.

'It's a silly name,' Laurie agreed. 'He doesn't look a bit like a monkey.'

'He's got monkey brains,' said Theo. 'I can tell. His name's Clinky Monkey.'

Clinky Monkey liked their house. He liked the boys. He slept on their beds at night. He played football with them.

Nobody had reported losing a dog that fitted his description, so their mum let them keep him.

Then, a few days later, this came on the local television news:

'Timothy Potts-Smythe, nine-year-old son of multibillionaire Frankie Potts-Smythe, was kidnapped from his home in Pembroke Road, Bristow, in the early

hours of yesterday morning. There are still no clues as to his whereabouts . . .'

'That's one of the big houses round the corner,' said Joe. 'I wish someone would kidnap me. It would be great!'

'So do I,' said Laurie, 'then I could have your cricket bat.'

Then a picture of the kidnapped boy appeared. He had long straight hair, glasses and big ears.

'Coo, what a geek!' said Laurie. 'Who'd want to kidnap him?'

When Timothy Potts-Smythe's picture appeared, Clinky Monkey jumped up. He barked and scratched at the TV screen.

'He seems to recognise him,' said Joe. 'Maybe Timothy is Clinky's real owner.'

'No,' said Theo. 'I'm his real owner because he's mine.' He stroked the dog's head. Clinky wagged his tail. 'See, he's wagging his tail because he's my dog.'

'I couldn't bear to give up Clinky Monkey now,' said Laurie. 'I love him. Mum's nearly forgotten she said we could never, ever have a dog. She likes him too.'

'But if Clinky *is* that boy's dog,' said Joe, 'we really ought to take him back. It's not far to Pembroke Road. Why don't we go for a snoop?'

2
Mr Cheeseman

It wasn't hard to find the Potts-Smythe house; reporters, sightseers, and cameramen had gathered in a big crowd outside it, waiting for news.

The children squeezed through to the front of the throng. A very large policeman was guarding the tall iron gates. He was standing in the full sun. Sweat beaded his face and hung off his moustache.

'Ooo! Fancy living here!' said Laurie, peering through the gates at the big house.

Theo was holding onto Clinky Monkey's lead. As soon as they got to the gates, the dog began to whine. He scrabbled at the ground as if he wanted to dig it up. He tugged on his lead.

Theo tried to hold him, but suddenly Clinky shot off like a rocket, pulling the lead out of Theo's hand. Clinky squirmed round the policeman's legs, squeezed through the bars of the gate, and scampered into the Potts-Smythes' garden.

'Oy!' cried the policeman, spinning round. 'No one's allowed in there!'

'Clinky! Clinky!' Theo shouted.

The people in the crowd stared at him.

'Hey, Mr Policeman, can we go in and get our dog?' said Laurie.

The policeman stared straight ahead. 'Nobody's allowed in there,' he said.

Theo cried louder: 'My Monkey!' he wailed. 'Clinky Monkey!'

Everyone was staring at Theo now.

'Poor little thing. What's the matter?' someone asked.

Theo pointed at the policeman with the moustache. He cried some more. 'Him!'

'Did that policeman hurt you?' asked a reporter, quickly snapping a photo of Theo. He grabbed his notebook to take notes.

'I never touched him,' said the policeman, sucking his moustache. He leaned over and whispered to Joe: 'Does he really think the dog's a monkey?'

'What? Er, yes,' said Joe. 'He's a bit, you know, funny in the head and we have to humour him, otherwise he gets really bad. Terrible. He can't be parted from Clinky, not for anything.'

The policeman stared down at Theo. 'He looks OK,' he said.

'I'm not OK,' shouted Theo. 'I'm nearly four!'

The reporter joined in: 'Ah, let the little lad in to get his dog, Officer.'

'Please,' begged Laurie. 'He'll never stop crying until he gets Clinky back.'

The policeman beckoned over a younger officer with a very red face. 'Take 'em in,' he said. 'Find that blooming dog.'

The crowd cheered as the red-faced policeman unlocked the big gates.

'Any idea what made him run off?' asked the policeman.

'It was a cat,' said Joe, nudging Theo.

'No, it wasn't, Joe!' sobbed Theo. 'Clinky thinks he lives here!'

Joe raised his eyebrows and made circles beside his head to signal that Theo was mad. 'Bonkers. Round the twist,' he mouthed silently.

There was no sign of Clinky Monkey in the garden.

The red-faced policeman led the three boys past the house, and over massive lawns that swept down to a turquoise swimming pool. Beside the pool, a tall thin man lay fully dressed on a sun-bed, talking into his mobile phone. He didn't see them coming towards him.

'Excuse me, sir,' said the red-faced policeman.

The thin man shot three feet into the air as if a bomb had gone off under him. His phone flew out of his hand.

'Excuse me, sir,' said the policeman again. 'I didn't mean to startle you. Are you Mr Cheeseman? The butler?'

Mr Cheeseman nodded. He had very yellow teeth packed tightly into a very small mouth.

'I'm PC Len Bartlett, sir, looking for this boy's runaway dog, Clinky.' He nodded towards Theo and winked. 'He's a bit, you know,' he added.

Mr Cheeseman stared at him blankly. 'What's the matter with you, Officer? Why are you making that face? Are you mad?'

'My Monkey,' sobbed Theo. 'Where's my Monkey?'

'See what I mean?' whispered the red-faced policeman.

'I don't know what you're talking about,' said Mr Cheeseman. 'What are you doing in this garden?'

Suddenly Clinky Monkey shot out of the bushes, dashed up to Mr Cheeseman, and snapped at his ankles. He barked furiously at him.

'Do you know this dog, sir?' asked the red-faced policeman.

'No.'

'Strange how he seems to have taken against you, sir?'

Mr Cheeseman glowered. His mouth got even smaller. He tried to push Clinky away with his foot. 'Never seen him before. Get him off!'

Then Mr Cheeseman noticed that Laurie was holding his mobile. 'What are you doing with my phone? Give it to me!'

'Sorry!' Laurie tossed the phone towards him.

'Mind the water!' Mr Cheeseman yelled. He lunged like a goalie, caught the phone, and fell flat into the pool with an enormous splash.

'Whoops, sorry,' said Laurie.

The red-faced policeman's face went even redder as he helped Mr Cheeseman out of the pool.

'Just an accident, sir,' he said.

'I'm going to strangle that little monster!' said Mr Cheeseman, clambering out of the pool. 'I'm going to—'

But the three boys had vanished.

3
The First Clue

The boys ran all the way home laughing.

'Well,' said Joe, when they got inside. 'It looks as if Clinky Monkey does belong to the Potts-Smythes.'

'No, he belongs *here*,' said Theo.

'Why d'you think Cheesyface pretended not to know Clinky?' asked Laurie. 'Clinky knew *him*.'

'Yeah. And he was really nervous, wasn't he?' said Joe. 'Guilty conscience, I bet.'

'Why?' asked Theo.

'I don't know – maybe *he's* kidnapped Timothy.'

'Hah! That's what I wondered,' said Laurie, 'so when I grabbed his mobile, I dialled 1471 to find out who'd called.'

'Mr Cheesy called,' said Theo. 'I saw him.'

'I mean, find out who called *him*! Then we'd have a clue.'

Joe picked up the house phone. 'What was the number that rang Mr Cheeseman, Laurie?'

Laurie told him and Joe dialled the number.

'Bristow Zoo. Mary speaking,' said the voice at the other end. 'How may I help you?'

'Sorry, wrong number!' Joe slammed the phone down.

'The *zoo*?' said Laurie.

Joe shrugged. 'Weird!'

The three boys watched the local news on television that night. The kidnapping was the main story again.

A ransom note had been delivered and the kidnappers were demanding six million pounds. The police were no nearer to finding the missing boy.

An expert from the Department of Handwriting and Forgery examined the ransom note.

'The writing has been cleverly disguised,' said the expert. 'We believe this was transcribed by a right-handed person using their left hand. The spelling is intentionally inaccurate. It's all a mess. A very, very clever piece of work.'

'That writing looks just like yours, Joe,' said Laurie.

'Ha, ha! What does that mean?'

'It means you wrote it, Joe,' said Theo.

'And it stinks,' went on the interviewer, wrinkling his nose in disgust. 'The smell is also a clue to who wrote this. An expert from the Ministry of Smells and Unexplained Aromas is investigating the pong, right now.'

'They don't know anything,' said Joe. 'I bet we can find Timothy Potts-Smythe before them. Let's go back to Pembroke Road, but in disguise, so no one will recognise us.'

'As cowboys?' suggested Laurie.

'Don't be stupid. No, I'll gel my hair back, that'll look cool with my shades. You can wear Dad's old beret and Mum's red scarf. With your striped tee shirt you'll look French.'

Theo could not be trusted to keep

himself disguised, so they left him at home.

On the way to Pembroke Road, Laurie practised his French accent.

'Bonjour, Monsieur Cheesyface! Eiffel Tower. Oo, la la!'

'I do hope nobody we meet speaks French,' said Joe.

There was still a crowd outside the Potts-Smythe mansion, though it was smaller than before. Unfortunately the same red-faced policeman and the same policeman with a moustache were on duty.

'Let's go round the back,' said Joe.

Just as they turned into the narrow side street behind the house, they saw the butler, Mr Cheeseman, climbing over the garden wall. He looked round furtively, then jumped down into the street and hurried off towards the local shops.

'He looks suspicious,' said Joe.

They followed Mr Cheeseman to a sandwich shop. He bought a peanut butter and jam sandwich on white bread.

'I wouldn't have thought that was his cup of tea,' said Joe.

'It isn't, it's his sandwich,' said Laurie.

'Ha, ha.'

Then Mr Cheeseman went into the sweet shop.

The boys sneaked into the shop too. The butler bought three cans of Coke, five packs of crisps and four bars of chocolate.

'He likes nice food, doesn't he?' said Laurie. '*Our* sort of food.'

They waited a few seconds after Mr Cheeseman left, so he wouldn't see them following him, then went after him. But he'd disappeared.

'That way, I think,' said Joe, turning up the road.

Suddenly a large thin hand shot out. It grabbed him by the collar and yanked him into an alley.

'Hey!' Joe looked round and found himself staring up into Mr Cheeseman's face. His heart sank. 'Uh, oh.'

The butler bared his ugly yellow teeth at him. 'Are you following me?'

'Bonjour, monsieur,' cried Laurie.

His navy beret had fallen across his forehead and with the scarf and striped tee shirt, he looked just like a miniature French onion seller. 'Bonjour.'

Mr Cheeseman let go of Joe. 'What?'

'Oui, oui,' said Laurie, smiling. 'Ah, bien, oui, oui, oui.'

'What?' Mr Cheeseman looked from one to the other suspiciously. 'Don't I know you boys?'

Joe beamed encouragingly. 'Oui.' He nodded and smiled. 'Bonjour. Oui.'

'You were following me,' said Mr Cheeseman, prodding Laurie. 'I saw you both.'

'Oh, la la!' cried Laurie, waving his hands about. 'Le Eiffel Tower, eh bien, oui, oui, oui. Eh, non, non, non.' He was desperately thinking of more French. 'Un, deux, trois. Le chat.'

'There's something not right here,' said Mr Cheeseman. 'You must know some English?'

'Speek Eeenglish? Pleeze?'

'Oh, forget it. Blasted foreigners. What did we win the war for? That's what I want to know. If I see you again, you're for it!' He spun on his heel and stormed off.

'After him!' cried Joe.

They followed the butler, ducking

behind bushes and hiding in shop
doorways. All the way past the shops,
past the park until at last he
stopped . . .

At the zoo.

4
Bristow Zoo

Joe and Laurie didn't have money to go into the zoo, so they went home to tell Theo what had happened.

'We think the kidnapped boy's in there too,' Joe told him. 'We'll have to go and investigate.'

'And you can't come,' Laurie added.

'I can,' said Theo. 'And Clinky Monkey can come too.'

'You can't take dogs into the zoo,' said Laurie.

'Clinky wants to come! *I* want to come!'

'Do shush, Theo. Actually, Laurie, you know it's not such a bad idea,' said Joe. 'If the Potts-Smythe boy is in the zoo, and Clinky *does* know him – and I'm sure he does, he'd smell him out.'

'And just how do we get a dog into the zoo?' said Laurie.

'Disguises again.'

'Yes,' said Theo. 'Clinky could be a tiger!'

'I've got a better idea,' said Joe, darkly.

That night when they should have been settled in bed, Laurie and Joe sneaked into Theo's room where the old baby clothes were kept in a big cupboard.

'Go away,' grumbled Theo. 'I'm asleep.'

'Shush,' said Joe. The cupboard creaked loudly as they opened it.

'Be quiet!' said Theo. 'You'll wake me up!'

'Sorry. We need things for Clinky,' said Laurie.

'Ah, here. Just the thing,' said Joe, pulling out an old babygro.

'That's mine!' said Theo.

'You're a big boy and big boys don't wear babygros, do they?'

Theo watched them suspiciously. 'Some big boys do,' he said.

Next morning they dressed Clinky Monkey in the babygro. He didn't like it. He didn't like the bonnet either; he tried to eat it. He was very embarrassed about wearing blue booties.

They strapped him into the buggy and snuggled a blue blanket round

him, and pulled the sunshade down
low over his head. They stood back to
admire their work.

'Brilliant. He looks just like any old
baby. Here are some choc drops, Theo.
It's your job to keep him quiet.'

'OK,' said Theo, eating a choc drop.

'Don't do that! They're dog chocs –
you might start barking.'

'Joe, if we do find Timothy,' said Laurie, 'won't we have to give Clinky back?'

'No, it's OK. We'll demand Clinky Monkey as our reward for finding him,' said Joe. 'I worked it all out.'

At the zoo, a coach had just pulled up at the gates. A large party of tourists from Wales was spilling out onto the pavement.

Joe carefully edged the buggy in amongst them. 'Pretend we're part of this group,' he whispered, 'otherwise they won't let us in.'

Laurie pushed in next to a large woman with glasses.

'What are you doing?' she said. 'You should stay with your mum.'

'Mum's gone back to the car for some nappies,' said Laurie, grinning. 'Sorry about the smell,' he added, pointing at the buggy and holding his nose.

The woman in glasses backed off.

At last they reached the turnstile. Laurie quickly started chatting to the boy beside him, Joe asked a mum what the time was, Theo ate choc drops and the lady in the kiosk waved them all through.

'We're in!' yelled Laurie. He sped off, pushing the buggy along at breakneck speed. 'Let's find Timothy!'

5
Timothy

There was a large map of the zoo near the entrance. The boys stopped to study it.

'Where's the most likely place that rich Timothy might be hidden?' said Joe.

'In the wormery,' said Laurie. 'He looked creepy. I didn't like his face.'

'It's being rich that makes you look odd,' said Joe.

'You must be a millionaire, then!' said Laurie.

'Ha, ha.'

'Joe, Joe . . .' Theo tugged at Joe's tee shirt.

'What is it?'

'It's Clinky – he's eaten – well, the choc drops are all gone. He wants to get out.'

'Well, don't let him.'

'But Joe!' Theo threw himself on top of Clinky. 'I can't hold him!'

'Is your baby brother all right?' A woman had been watching them and she came over and stared into the buggy. 'He seems very upset.'

'Go away,' said Theo, without looking round.

'You're going to hurt him doing that . . .' she went on. 'Let me see.'

'Oh, he's fine,' said Joe, wheeling the

buggy off rapidly.

'But he's making such a funny noise!' She followed them, trying to peer into the buggy.

'He has fits,' said Joe, remembering their granny's dog which *did* have fits. 'It's epi-epi-epileptricity. That's it.'

'Poor thing, epilepsy? Can't I help? I could . . .'

'Oh, look, there's Mum!' Laurie yelled suddenly. Grabbing the buggy, he spun it round and raced towards the flamingos.

'Phew! That was close,' said Joe. 'Thank goodness she didn't see Clinky's long black nose, then she really would have been worried.'

They wandered past the flamingos and spider monkeys to the bear enclosure. A notice said:

EXHIBIT TEMPORARILY EMPTY.

AWAITING ARRIVAL OF NEW BEARS.

Suddenly Clinky Monkey started whining. He wriggled and struggled against the straps.

'Hold him!' said Joe.

'Whoops!' said Theo.

Clinky somersaulted out of the buggy. He hurtled straight over the fence into the bear enclosure. He raced down the rocks and disappeared in the shrubbery at the bottom.

A couple standing nearby had seen everything.

The young lady took hold of her husband's arm. 'Did you just see a baby wearing a blue and yellow babygro leap into the bear pit?' she said.

Her husband scratched his head. 'I saw something, but . . . Boys? Hey, boys, what was that? We thought—'

'It was Clinky Monkey!' roared Theo. 'I want him back!'

'A *monkey*?'

'Yes,' said Laurie. 'Clinky Monkey

belongs to the zoo. We take it for walks and things. It's lost its mother. It's a norphan.'

'Yes,' Joe said, 'and our father works here and we help. I'm just going into the bear pit to get him back. I'm allowed to.'

The woman gave a high-pitched giggle. 'So silly,' she said. 'We thought it was a baby.'

'Ha, ha,' laughed Laurie. 'Ha, ha, ha. Goodbye.' He scooted the buggy off quickly. Joe and Theo ran behind.

'I want Clinky,' said Theo. 'Clinky Monkey!'

'Shush! I'll get him,' said Joe.

'Go on then,' said Laurie. 'We'll keep guard.'

They went back to the bear pit. When no one was around, Joe quickly climbed over the fence and over the rocks to the bottom of the pit. He scuttled over to the caves where the bears slept. It smelt horrible – of wet fur, rotten meat and bears' wee. He held his nose as he tiptoed into the dingy underground area.

'Clinky? Clinky?' he called softly.

There was a sudden scuffling and scratching noise and a soft sort of growling noise. Joe gulped. He stood very still. What if that notice was wrong and there was a bear in here? A big, bad-tempered bear?

He couldn't move. His heart started racing and thudding like a mad thing. Now there was something coming towards him, he could hear the pitter patter of claws on the rock . . .

'Clinky! There you are!'

Clinky wagged his tail happily, barked, then sped off again. Joe chased after him.

Hidden behind the rocks, was a large cage. Inside it a pale, thin boy with glasses and long hair sat on a box. He was reading a book, *The Secret Life of the Pygmy Hippo*.

The boy was Timothy Potts-Smythe.
Joe and the boy stared at each other.
'Hello,' said Joe.

'Hello,' said Timothy. He carefully
put a page marker shaped like a giraffe
into his book before shutting it. 'That's
my dog, Tufty. Some imbecile's dressed
him up in baby clothes.'

Joe wasn't sure what an imbecile was, but it didn't sound too good. 'It's a disguise,' he said. 'There's a six million pound ransom demand for you.'

'I know. I wrote it,' said Timothy.

'What?'

'I wrote it. Is it true the experts can't identify the smells? It's bears. They do pong.'

'What are you doing here?'

'Well,' said Timothy, crossing his legs, 'I arranged to be kidnapped. You see my parents are the pits, they won't let me keep a pet and I adore animals. My parents are super duper rich and what do they spend their money on? Holidays, useless yachts and fancy, la-di-dah schools, when they *could* buy a safari park and help endangered species. They *could* have their own zoo. They *could* buy me a cheetah or a baby elephant or a pygmy hippo.'

'Not many parents would do that,'

Joe pointed out.

'Nice ones would. Anyway, Cheesy, the butler, came up with this kidnapping lark. His friend Mungby works here. It's great in the zoo. I can stay hidden here *and* I get to see the animals.'

'But, your parents want you back.'

'Tough. They can't have me unless they give Cheesy and me three million quid – each.'

'But we've found you and come to rescue you,' said Joe.

'That's your problem,' said Timothy. 'Nobody asked you to find me. You won't get a reward from my parents whatever you do. They are *tight*.'

'I don't know what to say,' said Joe.

'Well don't say anything. Just leave me alone.'

'What about Clinky?'

'Do you mean Tufty? I had to keep him in the wardrobe because Mum and Dad won't let me have animals in

the house. Cheesy hated him – don't
think he liked Cheesy either. You'd
better hang on to him for the
moment.'

'Isn't it scary here at night, on your
own?'

'No, it's great. I walk about and talk
to the animals. I can, you know.'

'Can you? That sounds fun.'

'It is. Listen, there's only room for
one kidnapped boy here, so don't get
any ideas.'

'Don't worry, I won't.'

Joe tucked Clinky Monkey under his
arm and climbed out of the smelly
bear pit as quickly as he could.

6
Cheating Cheeseman

The zoo was about to close. The
three boys were sitting on a bench
outside the main gates eating ice
creams.

'When you think of that amazing
house and garden! The holidays and
yachts and things . . . what does Potty
Potts-Smythe want to sit in the zoo
for? He's got everything!' said Joe.

'He hasn't got everything,' said
Theo. 'He hasn't got me.'

'Not everyone would want you,' said
Laurie, making a face.

'And he hasn't got *you*, Laurie,'
Theo went on. 'Or Clinky, or Mum, or
Joe.'

'But he wouldn't want them.'

'But he hasn't *got* them, and we
have. We don't hide in zoos.'

'He's right,' said Joe.

'That's because I'm nearly four.'

'Shush! Look!' Laurie said suddenly. 'There's Cheesyface.'

They hid their faces with their ice creams. The butler kept looking at his watch. He was waiting for someone. After a few minutes, he was joined by a zoo worker dressed in green overalls.

'I bet that's Mungby,' said Joe. 'Wonder what they're saying?'

'I'm going to find out,' said Laurie. He wrapped himself up in the baby blanket. He squeezed himself into the buggy, pulling the sunshade down to hide himself. Digging his heels into the pavement he pushed himself backwards towards the two men.

Cheeseman and Mungby were so deep in conversation, they didn't notice the self-propelled buggy as it coasted up behind them.

'. . . they won't pay,' Cheeseman was saying, crossly. 'Stupid boy asked for

six million quid!' He snorted. 'And the fool thought I'd share it with him! Crazy kid.'

'He is sort of mad,' said Mungby. 'Says he likes it in there, talks to the animals. Listen, Cheeseman, the bears are coming back tomorrow—'

'The greatest scam of all time and the boy's ruined it,' Mr Cheeseman interrupted.

'Can't you make him ask for less?'

'D'you think I haven't tried? Wants his own safari park and must have three million. No. I give up. Let the bears in. He likes animals, it'll be a treat for him.'

'Cheeseman! They'll kill him!'

'Good. It'll save me the bother. Think about it, Mungby, if he goes free he'll tell. We'll be off to jail. So he's got to die. This'll look like an accident. Clever.'

The two men shook hands and went their separate ways.

Laurie went back and told the
others what he'd heard.

'Yikes,' said Joe. 'A real live murder!
We must warn Timothy!'

7
Saving Timothy

When Laurie and Joe went back to the zoo early next morning there weren't any crowds to hide amongst so they needed a new plan to get in.

Joe went up to the desk, smiling sweetly. 'Excuse me? My little brother lost his cuddly tiger here yesterday and he needs it back.'

'Oh-o-o,' wailed Laurie, rubbing his eyes. 'I want my cuddly tiger. Lickle tiger, he's my bestest animal.'

'Oh, dear, poor lamb,' said the lady. 'I'll phone through and see if it's been handed in.'

'Don't bother,' said Joe, quickly, 'we'll just nip in and get it.'

'I know where it is,' said Laurie. 'I dwopped it in the bushes by the cuddly lickle flamingos.'

Joe kicked him.

'I shouldn't let you in without your mum . . .' said the lady.

'She's just over there in the car with the, er, triplets,' said Joe, pointing vaguely. 'They're asleep.'

'Oh, triplets?' She peered into the street.

'Yes. This is the first time they've all been asleep for *sixteen* hours.'

'Sixteen? How does she manage? Is she . . .'

But the boys had vanished.

54

They raced round the zoo, screeching to a halt when they reached the bear enclosure. They stared down into the pit.

Two enormous shaggy brown bears were prowling around in the enclosure.

'Oh, no! Too late!' cried Joe. 'They've eaten him! We should've phoned the police. We should've told someone.' He sat down. 'Do they look as if they've just eaten him? Is there blood or anything?'

'No,' said Laurie peering into the pit. 'Oh, yes. Look. I can see a foot and look, there's a trouser leg!'

'Gross! I'm going to be sick,' groaned Joe, clutching his stomach.

'And I can see another leg and an arm and—'

Joe sprang up. 'What?'

It was Timothy – all in one piece.

'You pig, Laurie! I should punch you on the nose for that!' said Joe.

'Serves you right for kicking me.'

'Hey! Timothy!' Joe called. 'It's me. You've got to get out. Those bears are dangerous!'

'Hi!' Timothy called up to them. 'They won't hurt me. I can talk to animals.'

'Sure, 'course you can,' said Joe under his breath. Then more loudly: 'Come up here. Please? I've got to talk to you!'

'Oh, all right.' Timothy climbed up. 'You needn't have worried about me,

though I could do with a bath.' He sniffed himself. '*Bears.*'

'Poo! Smelly!' Joe agreed. They walked towards the lake. 'Listen, Potts, we overheard Cheesyface and he plans to get rid of you so you can't tell on him. He was going to take all the ransom money anyway. He wanted the bears to kill you. He said so.'

'I don't care. I'm not going home,' said Timothy. 'If my parents don't think I'm worth six lousy, measly million quid, I'll stay here.' And he sat down heavily on a bench.

'TIMOTHY!' It was Mr Cheeseman; he was coming straight for them.

'Whoops! Run for it!' Joe cried.

Timothy ran for it.

As Cheeseman sprinted up, Joe stuck out his leg. The butler tripped and flew over the low fence and into the lake with a tremendous splash. Ducks and weed and fish sailed through the air.

'Whoops!' said Laurie. 'That's the second time he's gone swimming fully dressed.'

Timothy headed to the gorilla house. Joe and Laurie followed him.

Cheeseman dragged himself out of the water. Weed clung to his head. Ducks quacked crossly at him. He climbed up the bank shaking water from his clothes and squelched after Timothy.

8
Mighty Max

Timothy looked weedy, but he could run fast. Before Joe and Laurie could reach him, he was inside the gorilla enclosure with Mighty Max, the massive silver-back gorilla.

'Oh, dear,' said Joe, pressing his nose against the glass.

'What if Timothy doesn't speak gorilla-speak? Then what?' gasped Laurie. 'The boy's bonkers!'

The gorilla stared at Joe and Laurie with its unfathomable black eyes and slowly peeled a banana.

Timothy began edging delicately towards Mighty Max.

A crowd of onlookers gathered. Zoo people arrived.

'Get out! Go back!' the zoo people yelled at Timothy. 'That animal is dangerous!'

Timothy gazed at them coolly. He waved them away.

'The boy's locked himself in,' said Mighty Max's keeper. 'Max is very fierce, very strong. Who knows what he'll do?' he added, chewing his nails.

Timothy inched up beside the great hulk of Mighty Max and put his arm on the gorilla's hairy knee. Mighty Max was surprised. He looked down at

the little pink hand, then up at Timothy. Slowly Max held out his great black paw and Timothy took it. He stroked it softly.

An old lady fainted.

Mighty Max put his mouth close up to Timothy's cheek – the audience held its breath – then the big gorilla, gently, gently nibbled Timothy's ear with his black rubbery lips.

The crowd breathed out.

Slowly, slowly, Max slid his huge arm around Timothy's narrow shoulders and clasped him to his massive chest. He squeezed him gently.

A young lady fainted.

'The boy's as good as dead!' cried the gorilla's keeper. 'Oh my God!' he added. 'There's another one in there! How'd that idiot get in? What's he doing?'

It was Mr Cheeseman. He was creeping up on Timothy with a look of pure hatred in his eyes, his yellow teeth bared in a snarl.

He didn't seem to have noticed Mighty Max at all.

A zoo official wearing a smart black suit appeared holding a large walkie-talkie. 'What's going on?' he demanded.

'That boy is called Timothy Potts-Smythe,' Joe told him. 'The kidnapped multibillionaire's son.'

'Oh, no!' said smart man, smacking his forehead. 'Why isn't he some crummy kid with poor parents who don't care about him? Why does this have to happen to me?'

'Perhaps you were horrid when you were little?' suggested Laurie.

The smart man scowled.

'And,' went on Joe, 'I suppose you should know that the other man is the kidnapper.'

'Better get the police,' said the gorilla keeper.

'Better get me some aspirin,' said

the smart man.

Mighty Max liked his new friend. He searched Timothy's head for creepy crawlies. He kissed Timothy's neck and sucked his ear. Timothy smiled and patted his knee and told him things in gorilla language.

Neither was aware that Mr Cheeseman was creeping up behind them.

The butler was so intent on watching Timothy, he didn't look where he was going and he stepped neatly into the middle of a dollop of gorilla poo. His foot slid out beneath him and he skidded across the floor on his bum.

'Whack!' He thudded heavily into Mighty Max's back.

Mighty Max jerked upright. His nostrils flared. His eyebrows rose slowly. Without turning round, he slid his arm away from Timothy and stood up.

He was much, much taller standing, than he was squatting.

Still he didn't look round.

He bared his large creamy teeth, growled low and deep and thumped his chest with his fists. Then he spun round, gathered Mr Cheeseman in his arms and swept him off the ground.

'Put me down!' yelled Mr Cheeseman. 'Put me – whoof!' The air flew out with a horrible wheezy gasp.

The gorilla squeezed him some more.

'Whoof!'

Mr Cheeseman began to go purple. His legs kicked feebly.

Mighty Max flipped him nonchalantly upside down and dunked his head in something horrid, then used his hair to wipe it over the floor. Next he grasped the hanging tyre and began to push Mr Cheeseman through the small hole in the centre of it. The butler was a tight fit in the small hole,

but Mighty Max wasn't bothered about that. He pushed and shoved and at last he got Mr Cheeseman wedged in. Then Mighty Max set the tyre spinning before sitting back down with his new little friend, Timothy.

The audience burst out clapping.

Mrs Potts-Smythe arrived. She knocked on the window.

'Timothy! Darling! Are you all right? Come out, come to Mummy!' she begged.

Timothy looked up slowly, as if he had all the time in the world and it was perfectly normal to be sitting holding hands with a very big gorilla in the zoo. He adjusted his glasses which had become a little wonky after the gorilla hugs.

'Oh, hello, Mummy.'

'Darling! Come out! Please!'

'I will, if you let me have a cheetah,' he said.

'Of course I will. Anything!'

'Promise?'

'Yes, I promise.'

'I'll have a pygmy hippo too, then.'

'Anything!'

Timothy whispered something into the gorilla's small hairy ear then got up and unlocked the door.

He fell into his mother's arms.

The crowd cheered. The television

camera captured the moment. A reporter stuck a microphone into his face.

'Timothy, that was a pretty amazing stunt in there,' he said. 'How did you get away from Mighty Max like that?'

'I told him he was on television and if he behaved himself I'd bring him some grapes. It's easy when you understand them. I understand them because I love them. Mum, stop kissing me. Mum, you promised me a cheetah and a pygmy hippo!'

'Yes, dear, yes, whatever you want.'

'Great, because if I have a cheetah and a hippo, I'm going to need a safari park to keep them in!'

'Oh, *Timothy*!'

That was almost the end of the adventure.

Mr Cheeseman was sent to jail and Timothy went back home with his family.

Joe and Laurie and Theo went to visit him with Clinky Monkey.

'We'll have to give Clinky Monkey back if Timothy wants him,' Joe said.

'I want to keep him,' said Laurie. 'He was meant for us.'

'I love him,' said Theo.

A new butler opened the door of the Potts-Smythes' grand house. He smiled as he showed the boys into the sitting room. He had nice teeth. He was a nice butler.

As soon as Theo saw Timothy, he rushed up to him with raised fists.

'You can't have Clinky Monkey!' he said. 'I'm going to hit you if you try get him!'

'You little bully,' said Timothy, backing off.

'No, I'm not, I'm a big bully!' said Theo.

'I must say I'm glad I don't have a little brother,' said Timothy, sitting down on a vast sofa, 'though you are

sweet.'

'I am not sweet!' yelled Theo. 'I want my dog.'

'Oh, you can have him,' said Timothy. 'I'm going to get my cheetah and my safari park, so I have to go to Africa. I'll be very busy. I can't keep Clinky.'

'What about his collar?' asked Joe.

'Oh, you can keep that.'

'But they look like real diamonds,' said Laurie.

'They are.' Timothy opened a drawer in the sideboard; it was brimming with diamonds. 'Never heard of the Potts-Smythe diamond mines? Lots more where they come from. Give me a lion or a tiger any day.'

'Me too,' said Theo. 'Or a dog.'

'Anyway, thanks for trying to help,' said Timothy. 'I love Tufty, I mean Clinky, too and I would have kept him if I wasn't going away. If you ever want a job in my safari park, all you have to do is ask.'

'The Potts-Smythe house is fantastic, isn't it?' said Joe as they went home. 'What great toys Timothy had!'

'What lovely diamonds!' said Laurie.

'That collar must be worth a fortune!' said Joe. 'Real diamonds!'

'No, you can't,' said Theo.

'No, I can't what?'

'You were going to say *sell it*. You can't. It's Clinky Monkey's and he likes it.'

'But Theo, we could buy thousands of collars with the money!'

'Clinky Monkey's the only dog in the whole of Bristow with a diamond collar,' said Theo. 'That's how I want it.'

And so that's how it was.

Read more books by the same author

THE TOAD PRINCE

by Rebecca Lisle

'A witty take on
The Frog Prince,
in which the princess
can't resist a suitor
who eats worms
and flies.'
SUNDAY TIMES

Trevor the Toad is in love with Princess Petunia,
but warty brown toads don't marry princesses –
unless there's a bit of magic involved.
Evil Wizard Wazp usually turns frogs into
princes, but when his clever dog Pong suggests
he turns a TOAD into a prince, he takes up the
magical challenge. Anything to impress the King!

What Wazp doesn't know is that clever Pong has
toadally tricked him . . .

THE TOAD PRINCE

£4.99 ISBN 1842703153

Read more books by the same author

Dogs Don't Do DISHES

by Rebecca Lisle

'Will appeal to
dog owners both
real and potential.'
BOOKS FOR KEEPS

'Just remember,' the inventor tells the Crumm family,
'although Metal-Mutt is made of metal and microchips,
he has a dog's heart and he needs walks and love too –
like all dogs.' But the Crumms are mean to
Metal-Mutt. They make him do all the cooking,
polishing, dusting and ironing. They even make him
do the children's homework. And they never take him
out. Or even pat his head. Poor Metal-Mutt. But then,
one day, he does something really brave and his life
takes a turn for the better!

Dogs Don't Do DISHES

£4.99 ISBN 1842703145

DAMIAN DROOTH
SUPERSLEUTH
ACE DETECTIVE

by Barbara Mitchelhill

with illustrations by
Tony Ross

Damian Drooth is a super sleuth, a number
one detective, a kid with a nose for trouble.
And here in this fantastic bumper edition are
three of his hilarious stories:
*The Case of the
Disappearing Daughter,
How to Be a Detective*
and *The Case of the
Popstar's Wedding.*

'Madcap cartoon-
sketch humour'
TES

9781849390972 £5.99

make friends BREAK friends

Julia Jarman

Daisy has two best friends, Phoebe and Erika, but they don't get on. Erika thinks Phoebe's feeble and Phoebe thinks Erika's a bully. Daisy has a plan to get her two best friends to like each other, but suddenly everyone is against her! Then the three girls have to spend a night together in a spooky old mill . . .

'Entertaining and realistic'
Julia Eccleshare, Lovereading

Gorgeously illustrated throughout by Kate Pankhurst.

9781849395090 £4.99

THE FACTORY MADE BOY

CHRISTINE NÖSTLINGER

Mrs Bartolotti is quite used to receiving surprises
in the post as she's very forgetful! But this one
beats the lot – Conrad, a perfect, factory-made
child who never does anything wrong.

But when the men from the factory realise that
the child has been delivered to the wrong address,
they come to take him back. Conrad doesn't want
to go so Mrs Bartolotti comes
up with a plan, and Conrad is
unrecognisable …

'Very funny … A surreal,
unusual story that's fun to
read and thought-provoking'
Bookbag

9781849394833 £4.99

AUNT
SEVERE
and the
DRAGONS

by Nick Garlick
Illustrations by Nick Maland

When Daniel's explorer parents vanish, he has to live with his strict and rather strange Aunt Severe.

But just when everything seems to be going wrong for Daniel, he meets four dragons hiding in the garden. They tell him about their lost magic book, The Spelldocious. But as soon as they leave the garden three of the dragons are captured by evil Gotcha Grabber, who throws them into his zoo.

With the help of Dud, a rather clumsy dragon, Daniel must try to rescue them and find the missing Spelldocious.

Nick Maland won the Booktrust Early Years Award and was shortlisted for Mother Goose Best Newcomer.

9781849390552 £4.99